The Western Contingent

Jesse L. Anderson

THE WESTERN CONTINGENT

DALKEY ARCHIVE PRESS
Dallas / Dublin

First Dalkey Archive edition, 2021

ISBN: 9781628972825
CIP Data: Available Upon Request

www.dalkeyarchive.com
Dallas / Dublin

Printed on permanent/durable acid-free paper

ONE

THEY SET OFF from Luan's central square on a clear-skied and dusty morning, parading two by two and due north along the town's principal thoroughfare while to the sides—cheering like the proud patriots they incontestably were—friends and family filled the air with breeze-snapped banners and the newly instituted flag of the people. Forty-eight young men drawn from the town and its surrounding villages, called upon by the nation for a task of the utmost secrecy and of the utmost importance. Leading them, a colonel and lieutenant colonel sent from the capital, field-proven fighters of impeccable repute whose show of confidence and poise that day helped to dispel—however fleetingly—the nagging fears of even the most nerve-racked relatives . . . The young soldiers were now nearing the halfway point between the central square and the town gate by which they would exit, causing the streets to become increasingly saturated with the ever-shifting spectrum of sound produced by the onlookers; by the moist-cheeked mothers letting out pained cries of affection and pleading with the colonel to look after their boys; by the fathers, relatively composed, shouting the requisite words, trite as they may have been, of wisdom and encouragement; by the screaming children who, whipped up into a frenzy by the ambient excitement, chased one another around their grandparents' legs; and, only really audible when the cheering subsided, by the voices and strings of the local musicians . . . Then—all too soon—the column of soldiers was filing through the ancient town wall's northern gate; the people of Luan surged forward in response, shoving and jostling one another to scream a final farewell to a brother or son, and the reigning decorum fell completely to pieces; and though the men at the vanguard were lucky enough to be spared the ensuing scene of lament, most of the young marchers found themselves leaving home in a state of panic and confusion, the hysteria around them growing and growing before being brought to an earsplitting head as the last pair of soldiers disappeared beyond the wall. Several minutes later—and mostly owing to the town elders and their words of solace—a relative calm had settled over the town. A few final and scattered wails served as a kind of conclusion, and then the people gathered up their dust-covered flags and began, slowly, to make their way home.

Several months earlier, while winter was transitioning into spring: without any prior notice, a liberationist messenger named Cheng had appeared on horseback outside the town gates and asked to meet with the local leaders. His request duly granted, he presented a decree directly issued from the newly appointed secretary of interior, sealed, stamped, signed, final. Read aloud by Cheng then looked carefully over by the town council. An honor or a punishment? The man from the capital insisted it was the former—a unique opportunity to make a meaningful difference in the war effort, to strike a much-needed blow to the counterrevolutionary forces. Yes, but why us? why our town? asked the council. Surely there were populations more suitable, more war-ready. But Cheng paid the argument no mind: the orders had come from the highest levels of government, and were not to be questioned. And so word was spread throughout the town: in two weeks' time, every childless man above the age of sixteen would begin training for a mission vital to the liberationists' success against the counterrevolutionaries. For the moment the specifics were classified, but the name under which Luan's forty-eight young recruits would march—and potentially fight—was written out several times in the decree and several times shouted proudly out by Cheng during the course of that first meeting: the Western Contingent. A name deliberated and decided upon in the capital and then brought out here to the provinces, a name that filled most of the townspeople with the same mysterious and humbling awe they'd first experienced several months earlier, when a stray fighter plane bearing unknown insignia had come humming in low over the wheat fields of Luan and then continued along its trajectory straight into a nearby hillside, exploding, and leaving behind it a thick line of stenchy, black smoke.

Twelve days later more men came from the capital, a small team—riding in two massive trucks—which consisted of the colonel and the lieutenant colonel, as well as several lower officers who would leave just before the end of training. The accompanying supplies were hastily unloaded—binoculars, backpacks, tents, guns, uniforms, and much else besides, some of it foreign-made, some sourced domestically—and then, with Cheng waving a friendly farewell from a passenger-side window, the two vehicles were speeding back down the dusty road on which they'd arrived; in a single afternoon a temporary training camp was set up south of the city wall over an unused stretch of stone-choked dirt, and Luan's forty-eight conscripts were told to present themselves the following morning shortly after sunrise. Over the subsequent weeks they would learn how to fire a rifle, how to pitch a tent, how to march in a disciplined and orderly fashion, and, most importantly, how to think in accordance with liberationist ideology. Provincial peasant boys that most of them were, it all took some getting used to, but—despite his occasional and seemingly unprompted outbursts of anger—they found the colonel inspiring and amicable, while the chance to fire a quality-made foreign rifle filled them with a sense of empowerment they hadn't thought possible; the weeks of training were soon speeding on by, and then before they knew it they'd reached their last day, and then their last hour, and then at last they were finished and ready to set off on their mission; the young soldiers were granted a single day of rest to spend with their families, and then the day after that came the morning of departure.

Though the opposing factions now fighting for control of the country were desperate to use every modern means available to wage their civil war, their armies and militias lacked any organic experience in doing so. This meant that more than a small share of military organization, nomenclature, and strategy was imitation, had been taken from secondhand sources (books, newspapers, hearsay) and then retooled to conform to local ways of thinking. Imported weapons of previously unimaginable power were mastered through trial and error; rankings were handed out based more on a title's euphony than its traditional meaning; battle tactics were borrowed from error-riddled translations of classic foreign novels; and chains of command inexplicably crisscrossed, oftentimes tangling into a feckless knot. The result: most of the country's inhabitants' first encounter with so-called modernity was through a clumsy and improvised attempt at employing advanced methods of warfare . . .

They set off on a clear-skied and dusty morning, filing through Luan's northern gate and into the fecund fields of winter wheat that surrounded the ancient city wall. Despite the pride they felt at having come through their months of training and having been deemed, by the colonel, as fit, ready for conflict, a collective sense of unease kept them quiet for the first few hours of the march, and not even the colonel's repeated attempts to boost morale were able to rouse them from their stupor. However, as the memory of their mothers' cries was steadily beaten away by the march's rhythmic stomping, spirits slowly began to rise, while fear, in turn, subsided—and then, all at once, with what seemed an impossible spontaneity, the entire Western Contingent broke out into loud, fearless, patriotic song. Their voices traveled unhindered across the boundless plain, and with each new chorus, verse, and note, their fervor reached greater and greater heights, their limited songbook acting in no way as an impediment, for they were more than happy to cycle endlessly through it . . . They were on at least their tenth rotation several hours later when—still singing with undiminished optimism—the dirt road forked, and their northerly course was redirected toward the cardinal point more befitting of their name.

They continued westward into the evening, and

then with sunfall came the pitching of tents, the lighting of fires, the preparation of dinner. They'd found a welcoming stretch of grassy field which, though by and large windless, was crossed at intervals by a southerly evening breeze that many interpreted, given the general direction from which it came, as a final message of encouragement from home. Their meal was accompanied by a continuous burble of ambient laughter, and, when they'd finished eating, the colonel enthralled them with timeless tales of heroic battles and meticulously worded parables that exposed the counterrevolutionaries for the cowards and traitors they truly were. They then sang a final song to round out the evening and went off to bed, the stars shining above like scattered grains of blazing rice. The Western Contingent slept oh so peacefully that first night out in the countryside, their souls warmed and their minds calmed by the predictable dreams of home: of a great aunt's New Year's cooking or a mother's tender glance, of a lighthearted debate between a father and a favorite uncle or a furtive farewell kiss from a sweetheart . . . A restful night for almost everyone, although at some point in the very early morning several soldiers were briefly awoken by the sound, it seemed, of someone violently vomiting at the camp's periphery.

Although the Western Contingent had been trained to think and to act as a unitary whole, it was still—of course—made up of individuals, each of whom had his own name, his own character, his own hopes and defects: the eldest four, who were all in the latter half of their twenties and stood out from the others due to several slight, but undeniable, signs of aging on their faces or in their hair—and who, despite their age, enjoyed little respect from their fellow soldiers, this being due to the fact that any man over twenty-five in Luan still without wife, and thus without children, likely suffered from some form of mental or social incapacity—were Ku, Yun, Shaochi, and Hongwen; they, in turn, were followed by a larger group of soldiers in the first half of their twenties, and among whom there were, among others, two Fas, a Biao, a Fuzhi, and another Yun; they, in turn, were followed by the youngest and most numerically dominant group, all still in their teens, many of whom looked as if they'd only recently reached the far side of puberty—they included a Paoshan, a Lihuang, a handful of Anchings, several more Biaos, yet another Yun, three Lungs, a Chengwu, and a dozen or so others whose names, with three important exceptions, don't merit mentioning. The three exceptions: first, Wei, the arrogant but well-liked son of a calligrapher, broad-shouldered and short-statured with a face that, from certain angles and in certain lights, looked vaguely deformed; second, pale-skinned Fu, fidgety, distraction-prone, born to—and spoiled by—a government official father; and finally, rounding out the trio, Po, a contemplative and intellectually endowed son of wheat farmers, whose handsome, head-turning facial features belied a deep-seated reserve. Wei, Fu, and Po—friends unlikely but friends inseparable for as far back as their young memories could reach.

Two more long days of marching and two more

idyllic nights spent out in the countryside, and then upon waking on their third morning away from home the colonel announced that the following day they'd be stopping in the town of Yongti to pick up more supplies and an as yet undetermined number of horses to help carry them. But tonight, the colonel told them gleefully, they'd be making a special visit, as he wanted to give his boys a little treat before they started on the more demanding stretches of their journey. A half day's march, and they'd arrive at The Glistening Soil, a first-class whorehouse, well-known and frequented by soldiers from every corner of the country. The older soldiers let out an enthusiastic cheer; the younger ones hesitated, shared nervous sidelong glances, and then did their best to match the ambient excitement.

Hurry up, Po, we're going! *No, I'm a little tired, I think I'll rest a bit and meet you guys later*. What are you talking about, Po? Come on, get up! Everyone else is already leaving! *I'm just kind of tired, I didn't sleep so well last night*. Sleep? You're talking about sleep when we're about to go get girls? *I said I'd come later*. Don't make us get the colonel, Po. He's not going to like the idea of someone abandoning his comrades. *I'm not abandoning anyone, I just want to lie down for a while and then I'll come later*. What's wrong, Po? nervous? never slept with a whore before? *It's not*—Are you a virgin, Po? Oh, come on, don't put on that face, we're only joking. Camaraderie, Po. No one's going to trust you if you don't come along. No one trusts a soldier who doesn't like girls. *It's not that I*—No one'll tell your mother, Po. Come on now, we'll carry you there if we have to. *Fine, fine . . . Just let me grab my*—Up we go, Po!

The Glistening Soil was an imposing three-story wooden building—lantern-lit and painted in foreboding tones of indigo and crimson—that sat entirely alone on a vast, seemingly endless plain, distant enough from the main road to make getting there inconvenient (its isolation was said to be a testament to the quality of its services) while close enough to ensure its visibility to potential customers at any hour of day or night. The Western Contingent had set up camp just next door, and as they were led under waning sunlight through the courtyard and into the main hall by two middle-aged women, they saw that they were the establishment's only clients for the evening. More women soon appeared—younger than the matrons, girls really—and the soldiers were led to the candle-lit tables scattered through the hall. Jugs of alcohol were brought out, and the soldiers, brimful of anxiety and giddiness as most of them were, began to hastily imbibe—rice wine chased with weaker rice wine, top-quality stuff, though most of the young men lacked the palate to really appreciate it. The colonel made a lengthy toast; the lieutenant colonel made a shorter one; all the while, more girls were coming out to mingle with the soldiers. And then came the food: braised pork, steamed riverfish, a variety of noodles, a variety of dumplings, an assortment of pickled vegetables . . . All of it accompanied, of course, by ever-increasing amounts of alcohol. The mood grew festive, the girls flirtatious; thighs were stroked, ears were whispered in; and though the food stopped coming, the alcohol went on arriving unabated. (At some point, several young men caught sight of the colonel vomiting into a vase in a shadowy corner of the cavernous room.) Girls began pairing off with soldiers and leading them upstairs—there were more men than women, some would have to wait their turn. As the hall emptied, the soldiers left behind exchanged awkward glances. A few, embarrassed, even tried to quietly sneak out of the hall and back to their tent. The colonel, however, now violently drunk, forbade anyone from leaving: Camaraderie, boys, we fight together, we fuck together. And so, by daybreak, every young man in the Western Contingent had had his chance with a girl from The Glistening Soil—even if some, due either to nerves or excessive intake of alcohol, had failed to perform—and the soldiers now lay sleeping on whatever surface had met the twin requirements of proximity and reasonable comfort when exhaustion had finally overtaken them, some in beds, some in tents, some on benches or chairs in the hall where they'd dined.

Handsome, bashful Po had immediately attracted the attention of several girls and was one of the first soldiers to be taken to bed that night. He went with reluctance, staring back at his table and meeting the envious glances of Fu, Wei, and several others, as the girl, one of The Glistening Soil's finest, pulled him by the wrist toward the staircase and then up to a third-floor bedroom. After a brief preparatory washing—during which Po had already begun to painfully tumesce—the girl shoved him backward onto the bed, mounted him, and took young Po's virginity while the drinking and debauchery, still in full swing, continued downstairs. Po, though nearly paralyzed with fear, managed to stay fully engorged throughout the ordeal and was even able to enjoy himself a little as he neared, and then reached, his climax. Rather than going back downstairs for another client, the girl stayed with Po until he was ready for a second go-around, and the two young lovers ended up spending the rest of the night in each another's arms—although Po, convinced as he was that he'd contracted some irremediable and organ-deforming venereal disease, only managed to catch one or two hours of fitful sleep.

Upon waking, a most gruesome discovery: the mutilated body of Hongwen, a socially inept soldier about whom there were rumors of mild retardation, was found near The Glistening Soil's back exit, his throat slit, his genitals severed and stuffed into his mouth. His corpse was still in uniform, and a dark stain had spread throughout the pelvic region of his pants. After an inspection of the body, the colonel stormed into The Glistening Soil, demanding an explanation and threatening to torch the building with the girls locked inside it, but his tirade was almost immediately interrupted by an abrupt wave of nausea that knocked him to the floor, where he began vomiting up whatever liquid was still left in his stomach from the previous night. When he'd progressed to dry heaving, the lieutenant colonel helped him back to his feet, reminded him of The Glistening Soil's purported connections to various warlords who'd be only too happy for an excuse to carry out some imaginatively lurid revenge on a group of novice soldiers, and then led him out the door. The Western Contingent burned Hongwen's body, and set back off.

The march to Yongti was marked by an undercurrent of disquiet, and aside from several theories about Hongwen's death that circulated among the soldiers—morphing and taking on added layers of complexity as they made their rounds—the Western Contingent walked in silence. They reached Yongti just before nightfall and set up camp on the city's outskirts while the colonel went into town to meet with his liaison and arrange the delivery of goods and horses for the following day. He returned several hours later, reeking of rice wine but relatively composed, and announced that everything had been settled: the animals and supplies would be brought to the camp in the early morning and then, as a show of liberationist strength and goodwill, the Western Contingent would parade through the streets of Yongti before continuing on their way. He ordered everyone to get a good night's sleep so as to be in tiptop shape for the local citizens; he finished by saying that he had more business to attend to with the liaison and then left the camp.

And so Hongwen's absence was filled by eight young horses—eight new members incalculably more valuable to the mission than the human being they'd replaced—and just as life was getting underway on the streets of Yongti, the Western Contingent came parading in through the eastern gate, their confidence moderately bolstered by the presence of the newly acquired animals. The colonel, in unexpectedly good form, marched alone at the front, waving an enormous liberationist flag and loudly enumerating the crimes and misdeeds of the counterrevolutionaries. It seemed that the public had been notified in advance of the parade, as the streets had been left entirely unobstructed—and yet the Western Contingent was met with hardly a modicum of enthusiasm: no patriotic song or dance, no cheering crowds or painted banners, no grateful smiles from smitten young women. Just indifference, confusion, sometimes outright hostility. Fu even received a phlegm-fortified gob of spit on the cheek from a slight, slate-bearded old man; the young soldier persuaded himself that there'd been a misunderstanding, wiped the mess off with his sleeve, and then carried on marching with his head slightly bowed. By the time they were halfway through the city, most of the citizens had stopped giving even a passing amount of attention to the parade. The soldiers now wanted nothing more than to hurry out of the western gate and be on their way, but the colonel—still at the front of the column, still shouting with undiminished vigor and swinging his farcically large flag—kept a slow and steady pace, forcing the soldiers to endure the people's apathy. Most kept their eyes directed firmly toward the ground (the embarrassment even caused several of the youngest, most sensitive soldiers to shed a swiftly wiped away tear) until finally, after what felt like hours, the Western Contingent found itself reentering the plain and leaving behind the unmoved citizens of Yongti.

I don't mean to criticize him, but . . . doesn't it seem like the colonel's been acting kind of strange? What are you talking about? *The way he was screaming this morning, that didn't seem a little unnecessary?* Unnecessary?! He was telling the people the truth about the counterrevolutionaries. If screaming was the only way for him to get his point across, then I don't see how it was unnecessary. *I know, I understand all that, but they didn't seem to care, or to even really be listening, and he seemed completely oblivious to that, like he couldn't see what was going on around him.* He's a patriot! He knows he's fighting for the right side, and if some uneducated village idiots don't show the respect they ought to, why should he let that affect his pride? *Village idiots? Luan's smaller than*—And besides, I saw plenty of people who were happy to have us there. *Fine, but what about the drinking? What about when he came back to camp last night and*—You're coming very close to treason, Po! If the colonel heard what you were saying right now I wouldn't be surprised if he had you shot on the spot! *Okay, okay, calm down. I was only asking.* He's a patriot, Po! And we're lucky to have him leading us!

A stretch of eventless days bled one into the other. The soldiers continued toward the west through mostly mild weather, camping come nightfall, drawing water from the local wells, enjoying the large supply of dried fish they'd been furnished with in Yongti, ignoring the colonel's increasingly reckless drinking, ignoring his incoherent alcohol-induced speeches (on the crimes of capitalism, on the counterrevolutionaries' cowardice, on the corruption of his contemporaries) and the obscure military songs he'd shriek out at random moments during both day and night. The landscape changed, trees replaced plain; they passed through villages where the always indifferent inhabitants spoke a throatier version of their own language; they went on dreaming dreams of home. Some were desperate for action, for a quick skirmish, just one chance to fire their rifle. Most, however, weren't. A week, two weeks—no one really knew, no one really counted. They were progressing: they'd be somewhere else soon enough.

A series of cracks dispersed the monotony: a series of cracks on a sunlit forest path, and then another, and then a series of soldiers fell to the ground, some screaming, some silent, while those still standing either followed their injured comrades into the dirt in search of protection or began to fire indiscriminately into the surrounding trees; the colonel, his voice suddenly and miraculously filled with that old confidence and clarity that had once won him his soldiers' admiration, ordered everyone to stop shooting, get low, and make sure that their rifles were pointed at anything but one another. But no more cracks came from the forest, and the screaming of the wounded soon became intolerable. Fearing further ambush, the colonel sprinted from fallen soldier to fallen soldier, made a rapid assessment of the situation, and told the lieutenant colonel to take two horses and lead a trio of the injured into the next village. A fourth—suffering from a deep stomach wound and rambling wildly on about something someone's mother had once done with a donkey—he shot mercifully through the head. He told everyone to start marching again with guns at the ready and eyes trained on the forest, and the Western Contingent left behind the untended-to bodies of its three former members.

Well within shouting distance of the point of ambush, the bodies of the lieutenant colonel and the three wounded soldiers put under his charge lay mutilated and meticulously arranged into obscene positions at the center of the trail. The crudely skinned cadavers of the two accompanying horses made a kind of frame around the scene, and a thick layer of blood had flooded the path and begun leaking into the forest. The colonel, fearing now not only ambush but an irrevocable decline in motivation among his soldiers, ordered them to run past their comrades with their eyes on the ground. But, of course, everyone peeked, and everyone, of course, immediately wished they hadn't. Spurred on by fear, they regrouped with unprecedented efficiency and continued together down the path, cursing the forest, and longing for the open fields of Luan.

They reached the next village without further incident but, shaken by the day's events and now deeply suspicious of their surroundings and the people that inhabited them, they continued on and set up camp soon after. The colonel then gathered everyone together and gave a rousing speech on the ineluctability of liberationist victory, on the sacrifices that must ineluctably be made to achieve it, on the ineluctable cowardice of counterrevolutionary battle tactics—he was in rare form, and his words filled the soldiers with a sense of great purpose, with understanding and acceptance regarding the unfortunate fates met by their friends and comrades. He stressed that if they made good time tomorrow they would reach the town of Duaiyang—a bastion of liberationist support—and then assigned teams of four to two-hour rotations of guard duty before retiring to his tent. A short while later, the sun not even set, he reappeared at the center of the camp, rifle brandished, and began firing back down the path in the direction from which they'd come, slurring out insults and provocations until he'd emptied his chamber; projectiles spent, he then projectile vomited onto the forest floor before being led back to his tent by two soldiers standing nearby.

An inspection of the colonel's stomach contents by a group of curious soldiers revealed a more than moderate amount of blood mixed in with his partially digested breakfast and lunch. Several confused and disgusted glances were exchanged, and though no immediate comment was made, a detailed description of the colonel's vomit had made its way around the camp before the end of the evening.

Duaiyang was built along the shore of an expansive lake, and as the Western Contingent trekked along the narrow ridge that led into town the next evening, the soldiers could see distant fishing boats crossing the sun-speckled water, could distinctly make out the barked instructions of a captain addressing his crew. Soon after entering Duaiyang proper, a member of the town council came rushing up and exchanged a few quick formalities with the colonel. And, just as the colonel had assured his soldiers, the town did indeed seem to be filled with enthusiastic supporters of the liberationist cause: small groups of children waved and smiled shyly before disappearing around a corner, while the men and women welcomed them with warm words of greeting and gratitude. The official took them to the city's central square, where an ad hoc celebration quickly took shape. A band arrived and began playing regional folk songs at one end of the square; freshly cooked food was brought forth by the hospitable inhabitants, along with bottles of homemade liquor, which were passed around, and then passed around again, and then again; and at some point, when the soldiers had already reached a middling stage of inebriation, a town leader gave a speech in which he praised the Western Contingent's bravery and commitment and promised them a special surprise the following morning. The evening's festivities were characterized by a clearheaded and pleasant drunkenness, and at night's end the road-weary soldiers were led away by the kindhearted citizens and given lodging in local houses.

Roused by their hosts and then led back to the square—where a mass of people had already gathered in a rough semicircle and remnants from the night before (shattered bowls and bottles, polished-off fish skeletons) sat in small tidy piles just beyond the periphery of the crowd—the Western Contingent was ushered to the front row to watch whatever surprise it was that awaited them; as they settled into their places, an unseen bass drum began beating out at a regular tempo and an enormous cheer rose up from the crowd. Two officials materialized before the spectators: the man who'd first welcomed the Western Contingent upon their arrival and another whom none of the soldiers could remember having encountered. Speaking by turns, they emphasized the great honor felt by their town for having the privilege to host such fearless and dedicated fighters, young men willing to risk life and limb—to sacrifice themselves as individuals—for the well-being of the nation and its future generations; the people of Duaiyang would long remember the Western Contingent's selflessness, and as a modest sign of their appreciation and as an unequivocal demonstration of their loyalty to the liberationists, they wanted to provide the soldiers with a little show, with a bit of entertainment to help carry them through the remainder of their long and arduous march. Another round of cheering started up at the back of the crowd and made its way toward the front as the people parted to let pass a small group of limping, haggard, naked men—five in total—lined up one after another and in turn followed by a massive woman, gigantesque, wielding a whip which she unceasingly sent flying into the men's backs. As they approached center stage, or what served as such, the officials took turns booting the men to the ground while the whip-wielder ordered them back to their feet so they could be knocked down once again. The repetitive kickings caused a paroxysm of excitement among the crowd; demands for death and accusations of counterrevolutionary collusion came from all sides. Seeing them now from a clear vantage point, the Western Contingent noticed one especially off-putting form of punishment (on top of the scar-checkered—and now freshly bleeding—backs, the black and blue faces, the swollen ankles) that the prisoners had been subjected to: through each of their scrotums, a piece of thick rusty wire had been inserted and then shaped and welded into an imperfect oval, in order, it seemed, to discourage self-removal. As the kicking continued, a donkey-driven, barrel-filled cart was led forth by a prepubescent boy who, after making his delivery, quickly ran back to wherever it was he'd come from. Two more men then emerged from the crowd—ordinary citizens by the look of it, nothing to set them apart from the dozens and dozens of other men standing throughout the square—and, each taking a handle, very carefully transferred one of the barrels from the cart to the ground. The demi-giantess seized the nearest traitor by the wrist and dragged him toward it; she stomped on the prisoner's already mangled ankles for good measure and then made several demi-giant strides backward; immediately, without a word, without a call for repentance or a litany of their anti-liberationist crimes, the two men tipped over the barrel and a honey-gold liquid went streaming across the prisoner's body. The hospitable locals, not wanting their guests to be left out on any of the pertinent details, informed the soldiers that the substance in question was cooking oil, brought to a boil just minutes before being brought to the square. While the first prisoner writhed about on the ground shrieking, the same form of torture was then meted out one by one to the other four, each man's cries adding a unique timbre to a tortured harmony that resounded over the howling, taunting, laughing crowd. When all five of them at last lay writhing side by side, burnt and still burning, a pair of small children, encouraged by the town elders, went racing up and took turns ripping out the rusted scrotal rings that adorned the traitors' now blistered genitalia. And that, it seemed, was the grand finale: the townspeople dispersed soon after, passing by the Western Contingent to say farewell and safe travels before continuing on their way home for a late breakfast.

A good portion of the soldiers, feeling physically sickened by the spectacle, had done their best to avert their eyes in such a way that—so as not to insult their hosts—they appeared to be watching, when they were, in fact, taking in only a minimum of the morning's events. Due to the arrangement of the crowd, this meant that a large fraction of an already large number of the Western Contingent found itself looking almost directly at the colonel, upon whose face there was an expression so vacant, lifeless, and suggestive of insanity that not even the most imperceptive of soldiers could fail to see that there was something terribly off.

What do you think they did? Obviously something very bad. *Sure, but what? Do you think they killed somebody? stole something?* They were counterrevolutionaries. That's a serious enough crime in itself to justify what happened to them. *Why?* Why?! Why are you asking so many questions? *Why couldn't they just be put in jail?* Counterrevolutionaries, Po. They were ideologically tainted and a couple months in jail wouldn't have made any difference. They would have gotten out and started right back at what they'd been doing before. *And what were they doing before?* I swear, Po, if you keep this up—*I'm just asking. You aren't curious why someone deserves to have boiling oil poured over his body?* They were counterrevolutionaries, that's all that matters. *And what makes someone a counterrevolutionary?* That is such a stupid question, Po. *Yeah, well, I don't think you have a good answer to it.* A counterrevolutionary is anyone who's not a liberationist. It's as simple as that, and besides, it's none of our business. If Duaiyang wants to kill its own people that's got nothing to do with us. *Except that they killed them for our entertainment.* It's a war, Po. People are dying all the time, everywhere. Do you want to try and explain it? *Fine, fine . . .* We just have to keep marching and get where we need to be. That's all that matters.

Most of the remaining day was spent along the lake, and then toward sunset the path branched off from the water's edge and continued through the forest, where—the ambush still very much on everyone's mind—they spent a series of anxiety-ridden though ultimately eventless nights before happily emerging into a sparse, grassy, gently rolling landscape. On their first evening back out in the open, the colonel announced—as a tremendous storm took shape behind him, each crash of thunder resounding like a giant, shattering porcelain vase—that they weren't more than a three-day's march from the Sanyi River, a prominent and well-known waterway about which all the soldiers had heard stories during their childhood. They ate a hurried dinner and then, fearing rain, hid themselves away in their tents . . . The Western Contingent had fallen fast asleep by the time the storm finally passed over their camp, loud and luminous and all the rest, stealing a quarter hour's worth of sleep from most of the soldiers and a night's worth from the most shaken. Come morning, they discovered that one of their tents had been struck: burnt and crumpled, four dead comrades still lay inside it, still tucked snuggly into their sleeping bags.

Through a field of brilliant blue flowers, over the top of a meager hill, and then the Sanyi River came into view; a swift, effortless descent, and they then found themselves at a soft and sandy shore. But the river's size and the surrounding scenery left the soldiers underwhelmed—they'd been expecting more: more water, a bit more visual variety. The colonel, however, was ecstatic. He made a broad, sweeping gesture with his hand as if there were something magisterial to be taken in, and started on about the greatness of their country, of its unfathomable physical vastness, its uncountable cultural achievements, the irrepressibility of its people's endeavoring spirit. Those who survived the war and took part in the subsequent rebuilding of the nation, he promised, would see this greatness brought to a level heretofore unattained by any civilization in recorded history. A small group of soldiers watched the colonel, listening attentively, respectfully, while most tried to ignore him and hide their annoyance at having to attend to yet another histrionic display of patriotism. But as the colonel carried on, his voice began to fluctuate—a sentence that began on a note of dead seriousness would veer midway toward what could only be described as sarcasm, before coming to a close in wooden neutrality. The result was a strange but hypnotic half-song that caused the soldiers, curious to see where all this might be leading, to huddle in closer around the colonel. He spoke faster and faster, his tone grew increasingly erratic: each individual word was soon imbued with a distinctly different emotion and whatever literal meaning his rant might have had was rendered superfluous by the unhinged melody that contained it. Then, midsentence, he went silent and pointed up the Sanyi. Follow the river west, he soberly told his soldiers, and they would arrive where they were needed in some three or four weeks' time. He threw down his backpack, stripped down to his undergarments, and waded out into the river—a big smile, a big wave good-bye, and then he sank into the water and let the current carry him away, back toward the east.

TWO

THEY SET OFF from the riverbank and continued toward the west, hesitant and confused, a sense of aimlessness now weighing on their psyches. They'd watched in silence as the colonel had floated away down the not-so-mighty Sanyi and remained silent for a long while after he'd drifted out of sight—no one knew what to say, no one understood what had happened, and everyone was trying to come to terms with the overpowering dread that had taken root in the wake of the colonel's desertion. They felt like children waking up in an empty house, parents and elder siblings having inexplicably vanished. Finally, a soldier named Yun, who up till then had done nothing whatsoever to set himself apart from the Western Contingent's thirty-six other surviving members, stated matter-of-factly that they should get on their way, that there was no point in sitting by the river sulking, that when they arrived where they were needed everything would make more sense, and, besides, what else is there for us to do. A few grunts of agreement and no objections, and so they gathered up their things and started back down the trail, with Yun now acting as de facto leader of the orphaned soldiers . . . The path hews reassuringly close to the river, winding here and there to skirt around some minor shift in elevation, but never straying so far from the water that the soldiers lose a sense of where it is, while the sky, covered over with a vast expanse of thin, disheartening, sun-bleached cloud, acts as an unwanted counterpoint to the Contingent's collective mood. Conversation is dominated by hypotheses about the colonel—is he a traitor? a lunatic? what about the alcohol? what about his blood-tinged vomit? Hypotheses but little to no direct criticism: in the soldiers' minds the colonel's departure was somehow beyond his control, was just another one of the war's many casualties. The consensus eventually reached is that the colonel wasn't quite crazy—the word feels too strong—but that he'd simply seen too many young men die in his long and decorated career, and that this had finally caused something in his mind to come unraveled. (*I told you there was something wrong with him*. Shut up, Po. I'm not in the mood right now.) The conversation then moves on and several soldiers—an older Biao, a younger Biao, and a doctor's son named Fa—begin wondering aloud why they're going on with this, as they see it, already botched mission, and aren't starting back toward Luan. Why not follow the colonel's lead and head east—though by land, of course, instead of water? A small group of soldiers reminds them of their duty to the nation. A larger group reminds them of what happened in the forest. Someone adds that the people and villages along the Sanyi River are purported to be enthusiastic supporters of the liberationists and so it's safest to keep moving west as planned. Biao, Biao, and Fa remain unconvinced but quickly fall quiet in the face of so much resistance. Come evening, the soldiers set up camp on the flattest stretch of ground that they can find; come morning, Biao, Biao, and Fa have disappeared, as have three of the horses. Yun announces that anyone who so much as mentions the possibility of turning back will be shot. And then back to marching . . . Three days later, in the early afternoon, they began passing by scattered groups of houses—though there was no sign of the people who lived within them and the farmyards without were conspicuously empty—and realized they were on the outskirts of a town, which could shortly thereafter be made out in the distance. The Western Contingent felt a rush of excitement, not because they anticipated anything in particular from the town or its people—although a growing number of soldiers were becoming desperate for a woman—but simply because it was a change, a little diversion from the unvarying scenery on this stretch of the march. They found themselves moving almost unconsciously faster as they came closer to the town, and when they reached the outermost row of houses they at last saw a first sign of life: a small shirtless boy, ribs protruding and stomach distended, sat on the ground picking with chopstick-thick arms at grass and weeds, which he would roll into a ball and then place into his mouth for an extended and no doubt unpleasant chewing. He seemed oblivious to their presence, not once looking up from his foraging to meet the eyes of the soldiers, and as the Western Contingent continued down the street and deeper into the the town, they realized that the boy was only a harbinger of a more wide-ranging problem: skeletal women, summoned by the unfamiliar sound of robust young men tramping past their houses, came rushing out of front doors and latched on to the soldiers' uniforms, begging in a nearly incomprehensible dialect for a handful of rice or wheat, anything, whatever they could give, our crops have been flooded, our children are starving, there's not a single living animal in the entire province, while close behind them followed sons and daughters of various ages suffering from the same corporeal diminution as the grass-eating boy. (*Can't we give them something?* You can give them your own rations if you're feeling charitable, but I doubt it'll be enough to feed the whole village.) A gentle shove sufficed to keep the women at bay while the children by and large ignored them, not bothering to ask for even the smallest morsel of food—and just as the soldiers' excitement while approaching the village had precipitated a brisker pace of marching only minutes before, so now did their discomfiture lead to a hastening of steps. They quickly reached what seemed to serve as the town's central square, and it was there that they found the local men sitting in small circles and smoking stale-smelling tobacco. The soldiers stopped and looked them over, but every last local eye was fixated on the Western Contingent's five remaining horses . . . A group of six men, large, burly, no evidence of the famine on their muscled bodies, stands up and begins moving toward one of the animals; the closest soldier meekly asks what they're doing but the men ignore the question and knock him into the dirt. Yun shouts at them to keep their hands off the horse but again comes no response. They surround the horse and—as Yun moves toward them screaming out that they're about to steal government property, a crime which he assures them is punishable by death—start leading it in the direction of a nearby alley. Yun goes on shouting while several other soldiers make half-hearted attempts to pull the men away, and after these several soldiers are pushed aside (as easily, it might be mentioned, as the malnourished women they themselves had pushed aside before reaching the square), another group of local men decides, well, if it's as easy as that, they wouldn't mind having a horse of their own—a decision which is also soon reached by most of the other men on the square. Yun then reminds the Western Contingent that, without the horses and the supplies they carry, we're all going to shrivel up and die in this backwater shithole province: no better motivation than the deferral of death, and the bravest soldiers now make a concerted effort to stop the thieves, which leads to three of the Western Contingent's bravest soldiers getting a knife to the stomach or to the throat, which in turn leads to a general panic and a discharging of rifles . . . The young men stood scattered throughout the square, their eyes wide and their breathing heavy, guns still pointed toward the dozens of bullet-stricken locals—some dead, some moaning—waiting for some reason to do something, anything, else. Hardly ten seconds had passed, it seemed, before terrified, shrieking women began streaming in from all directions onto the square, leading the soldiers to conclude that it was best to leave. As they filed haphazardly away, they realized that two of their youngest members had also been shot, one of whom, a farmer's son named Lung, was still alive and perfectly cognizant of his surroundings—he pleaded with his passing comrades to set him on a horse, but owing to the ambient confusion and a seemingly self-spawned rumor being whispered from soldier to soldier that he was only minutes away from death and there was nothing to be done for him anyway, he quickly found himself sitting alone in the dirt, vainly trying to get back onto his feet and desperately praying to be back with his friends. The Western Contingent found a way out of town easier than they'd anticipated and kept a brisk, steady pace until the last outlying house had fallen well out of sight. And that was enough for the day:

they pitched their tents, ate their food, and then most of the soldiers went to lie down hours earlier than usual. (*What a pointless waste of life*. Go to sleep, Po. *You can sleep after that?* We're in the middle of a war, things don't always go as planned. *Did you shoot anyone?* We can talk about it tomorrow, I'm tired.) Late the next day, on a stretch of road running right along the river, the soldiers began encountering small groups of starving locals moving with what little strength they could summon in the opposite direction. More often than not they seemed to be composed predominantly of members of the same family—sometimes with two generations represented, sometimes three, once even with a possible fourth—but there were also trios and quartets consisting solely of young men, and even the occasional pair of wide-eyed children, little brother hand in hand with big sister, one skinny twin piggybacked upon another. Some of the passersby looked relatively healthy, their bones lined with the usual amount of muscle, while others appeared to be only days away from death; sometimes they stopped to stare as the soldiers strode past but rarely did they make any pleas for charity: either they'd staked all their hopes on wherever they were going or they knew that the soldiers would be of little help. Once, when a family in particularly bad shape came staggering down the road toward the group of soldiers, Po, overcome with pity, turned his head and fixed his eyes on the river, whose current just seconds later carried past the bloated corpse of what he took to be a young woman; he stared, only half registering what it was he was looking at, and followed the body with his eyes until it floated away around a bend in the river . . . The people keep on streaming past well into the evening and then shortly before sunfall the Western Contingent comes to a village built on a steep incline rising up from the water. A path branching off from the river allows them to maneuver around it, but in the lingering evening light they're able to look down from their unfortunately clear vantage point straight into the heart of the village, where people lie or sit in various positions—against walls, in the center of the street, on random objects serving as chairs—dying or already dead. Several soldiers wonder aloud why they don't at least have the dignity to go die indoors, why they have to be out here flaunting their misery for all the world to see, questions to which Yun provides a reasonable response: likely they're not from here, just look at how many of them there are, likely they've come from someplace else hoping for some last chance of survival in the next village, or the one after that, or the one after that, and when their hunger becomes so great that they lose the will to keep trying, they set themselves down wherever they happen to be and wait for consciousness to fade to black. They set up camp at a safe distance from the village, and after a large, hearty meal of rice and dried fish, Yun assigns a rotation of soldiers to watch duty for the night and the Western Contingent goes to bed with a whole new set of images to trouble their sleep. (*Why are we going this way? why west? All the fighting's in the south, what could there possibly be for us to do out here?* People are saying that the counterrevolutionaries are responsible for the famine. The locals need to see that we're here for them, that there's still hope. *Why would the counterrevolutionaries starve all these people? What could they gain from that?* Their motives are—*And what do you mean by hope? Without a miracle, these people will all be dead before the end of the month.* Everyone has to make sacrifices. At least if they see how strong and proud we are, how strong and proud the liberationist side still is, they'll die with the comfort of knowing that the future of our country is in good hands. *I'd say they're too busy wondering where their next meal is going to come from to be contemplating the future of the country.* Everyone has to play their—*Never mind. Forget I said anything.*)

Over the days that followed, the itinerant famine victims began passing by with increasing frequency and were often grouped together in greater numbers: it wasn't unusual to see groups of ten or twenty or even thirty moving together through the countryside, the relatively strong supporting the absolutely weak, feeble-bodied teenagers helping along feebleminded grandparents. Corpses and soon-to-be corpses lying at the edge of the road or just beyond it became an all too common sight, and sometimes whole families who had resigned themselves to the inevitable huddled together in the surrounding fields, holding each other and taking turns dying. The catastrophe had blanketed the region with a peculiar smell whose strength fluctuated throughout the day, and although it was by and large horrifically off-putting, with a deep enough breath, taken at the right moment, unexpected and pleasurable notes could be detected within it; it caused some nebulous memory to crop up in Po's mind, which several minutes of concentration succeeded in giving form to: one evening, in the home of his maternal grandparents, an uncle had recounted the time he'd sampled a notoriously foul-odored tofu while traveling through the southern provinces, which had smelled, he'd said, like rotten pork belly stewed in plum juice—a description that was also fitting, it seemed to Po, for the odor of mass death. More days, another week, more nights spent out in barren fields; there were more villages, more towns, each one more deserted than the last. Soon, the only signs of life to be seen were out on the road, but even there the proportion of living to dead was beginning to decline; it wasn't long before the latter outnumbered the former, and it didn't take much longer after that for the still breathing, let alone perambulatory, to become a singular sight. (*There are so few of them left now, can't we at least help the ones who look like they still have some chance? There's no reason not to spare a little rice.* You'd only be prolonging their suffering. If you really want to do them a favor, better to be generous with your bullets than with your food.) They encountered stretches of road so dense with death that even with the most careful of guidance from the soldiers a horse would inevitably send a hoof through some cadaver's hunger-enfeebled torso. Either entire villages had begun dying en masse or the near-to-death had decided it best to die alongside the already dead—whatever the case, the higher concentration of bodies and the arrival of an early summer heat wave were causing the pork belly and plum stew-redolent stench to grow in both pungency and complexity. When it became too strong the more nausea-prone soldiers could spend hours at a time sporadically vomiting with an intensity worthy of the colonel's sloppiest evenings, collectively bringing up enough half-digested and still nutrient-rich food to feed a family of five for several days. It was as if the smell had embedded itself in the very ground, had become as integral a part of the landscape as the unyielding, worthless fields that sat to either side of the path; the Western Contingent could march for an entire afternoon without encountering a single corpse and still the smell sat heavily on the air, undiminished, as if minuscule pieces of decomposing flesh had got caught in their nose hairs. The soldiers would deem it intolerable one hour only for it to become more intolerable the next, and then even more so in the hour after that. Each day there were fewer and fewer bodies on the road, and yet each day the smell was there, as pervasive as it had been a week before, interfering with sleep and causing bizarre dreams in which food and human forms came together in terrifying amalgamations. A theory was spread throughout the Contingent that it was coming from the west, that they would soon be encountering enormous piles of bodies, unending mountains of them, that there was no other possible explanation for the smell's tenacity than an unthinkably large source farther up the road. Either that, or it was all a big joke being played on them by some superior power—be it earthly or divine—or, then again, perhaps it was simply a group delusion, we've been traveling together long enough for that to happen, don't you think? like sisters who always start their periods on the same day? (This isn't going to end, is it? We're going to be walking through this stench until we run out of food and end up starving like those people back there. We should have turned back when we had the chance. *I see that fear has taken the place of patriotism.* There's nothing patriotic about us dying out here without having seen any real fighting. *War, Wei. Like you said, it doesn't always go as planned.*) And then, like the sky banging together its hands, black clouds came tumbling in one early afternoon, bringing with them a storm: not having forgotten the outcome of their previous encounter with heaven-sent streaks of electricity, most of the soldiers—with thudding hearts and shaking hands—spent the hours that followed anxiously tracking the lightning's progression, pleading with it to keep its distance. Which it mercifully did. And when the sky cleared and tensions eased and the soldiers were once again breathing in and out through unpanicked airways, the realization quickly set in that the land had been purified and the smell of death washed away. A cause, of course, for celebration: a cheer went up and, with a spontaneity not seen since the earliest days of their march, the Western Contingent broke into song, and though the words they sang may have been dramatically out of keeping with the meager amounts of pride and confidence they presently had in their mission, they belted them out with all the mindless enthusiasm of neophyte soldiers. They went on singing throughout the afternoon along the rain-muddied road, and that evening, with nothing now to hinder their appetites, they allowed themselves a feast of irresponsible abundance and then went to bed festively late, their heads spinning with happiness and rice wine . . . Two days later: a small wooden cabin sitting alone at the edge of the Sanyi comes suddenly into view as the Western Contingent passes over the crest of a hill. It's not much more than a minute's march away, and as they approach and their point of view shifts, the soldiers at the vanguard notice a meager, rotting dock near the building's back door: a boat floats at the end of a tautened rope, and there appear to be several figures stretched out at the waterside—minds immediately imagine corpses, and after their brief streak of days during which death had begun to seem increasingly distant, it's only natural that the soldiers, their pace now slowing, feel an acute pang of disappointment. Then the barrel of a gun smashes through a windowpane, a shot is fired, and half of Yun's head is transformed into a stain on the uniform of the soldier standing behind him. Rendered once again leaderless and now under fire, the soldiers react in one of three ways: by shooting back, by dropping to the ground, or by retreating up the hill. And although retreating proves to be the most prudent choice if short-term survival is foremost on one's mind, the soldiers who opt for it are mentally marked by their comrades, causing an as yet unnoticed schism to splinter through the Contingent. . . After Yun, another seven soldiers had been gunned down—only one of which went on breathing for more than several minutes after the exchange—and though no one dared to mention it, panic-blind friendly fire had made a clear contribution to the gratuitously high body count. The eastern wall of the cabin was shot through with holes of every size, and through one of the most gaping could be discerned the top half of an obese man lying flat and still on the wooden floor, an almost comically large rifle tucked with post-coital tenderness into his arms. The soldiers approached with caution, guns at the ready; and as they did, they became aware of a smell not unlike the one that had haunted them for so many miserable days, which, though not an exact replica, was most certainly a reinterpretation of the same material, made up of the same major components but mixed in different proportions. Some gagged and stopped where they stood, but the curious and stomach-strong continued toward the source. The figures out back were indeed dead bodies, or, more accurately, the remnants of dead bodies, bizarrely butchered, missing muscle and flesh and internal organs, while inside the cabin, forming a backdrop to the fat man's grotesque and bullet-riddled corpse, was another set of bodies, a dozen at least, stacked in a row on the floor or pierced through with meat hooks that hung from the ceiling, some intact, others nearing a state similar to those by the river. Nothing to be done, no further justice to be had. Several soldiers gave blunt little kicks to the head of Yun's killer as they left the building, but it gave them scant satisfaction. On our way then? The Western Contingent started unceremoniously back down the road, leaving behind them the bodies of strangers and friends and feeling relieved when the last lingering reminders of death had vanished from the air.

THREE

Po woke up that night to the sound of shouting: shouts of hate, shouts of pain, and shrill pleas for reconciliation.

He sat up, saw Fu sitting up beside him, saw that Wei and Paoshan had already left the tent; the two friends cautiously peeked outside, saw soldiers being dragged by soldiers in the moonlight, saw other soldiers trying to intervene.

It seemed that—besides the two of them—the entire Contingent was taking part in the conflict, and based on the movement of certain arms and the pitch of certain screams, Po deduced that knives had been drawn and were being zealously put to use.

Those doing the stabbing shouted out accusations of cowardice and betrayal.

While those being stabbed shouted out a blend of apologies and denials.

Po made a sideways glance at Fu, met Fu's already sideways-oriented eyes.

What should I do? *Did anyone else see you go up the hill?* I have no idea. *If they didn't drag you out with the others, I think you're safe. If anyone asks, though, I'll say you were with me the whole time.*

Po took a first step outside the tent, was simultaneously arrested by the sound of gunfire and Fu's sweat-beaded hand wrapping around his upper arm, if you go out there you'll only draw attention to me.

Another round of gunfire, and then a respite.

And then a crescendo of shouts, and then more

gunshots; then several last stabs into already inert bodies—prompting several last grunts and groans—and then it was over.

The soldiers who'd tried to stop the act of retribution shoved and swore their way back to their beds while the others debated what to do with the corpses.

Did they deserve a burial? a collective cremation?

No: after all, they'd abandoned their duties, proven themselves worthless in battle.

And so: further punishment? a little postmortem mutilation? gelding? a cutting of throats and tongues?

No: after all, they'd once been comrades, they merited at least a modicum of respect.

And so: the bodies were dragged away from camp and left stacked together at the base of a tree.

The body count: nine—leaving the Western Contingent with twelve soldiers.

When Wei came back to the tent, dirt and blood comingling on his bare torso, he told them that Paoshan was dead and we're all going to go wash ourselves off in the river if you—and his eyes fixed on Fu, and perhaps too hastily Po asked what was the matter, and Wei looked to the side, said that nothing was the matter, and then finished his invitation.

Which they declined, claiming fatigue.

He knows. *He doesn't, he's just tired and he got distracted*. I don't trust him. *Neither do I, but he'll believe me if I tell him you didn't retreat*. What if someone else saw me? *Paoshan didn't go up the hill*. What? *He was next to me, shooting back*. Are you sure? *Yes*. You don't think they got me confused with him, do you? *I don't know*. You think I'm a coward, don't you? *Of course not*.

When later they heard the return of the riverbathers, Po and Fu fell silent, tucked themselves into their sleeping bags, and began to feign sleep—several rounds of laughter issued from outside, and then Wei entered the tent and was laid out and loudly snoring before Po's heart had had time to regain its normal rhythm.

And in the morning, although he'd no doubt had a nearly sleepless night, Fu could still be counted among the living, and had the privilege of continuing the march alongside his comrades . . .

Two days after the purge, the trail, which had begun leading the Western Contingent into higher elevations, brought them to an immense waterfall, with an enticing pool—ideal for swimming—rippling below it.

Pine trees grew at improbable angles across the cliffs encircling the site.

The white-capped mountain range they'd first

caught a small glimpse of the day before now sat fully exposed in the distance.

And the sun, hovering high in the sky, cast a wheat-colored glow over the rocks and the leaves.

A little grove of tranquility for the road-weary soldiers.

Maybe we should sleep here for the night.

There then followed an afternoon and evening of much-needed rest and idyllic diversion, of swimming and splashing and carefree fun; and of course a roaring campfire to round out the day—with the requisite singing and drinking and exchanging of stories, and a good deal of reminiscence over dearly missed Luan—before the Western Contingent went off to bed and was lulled to sleep by the soothing sound of water meeting water.

But . . .

Upon waking, a most gruesome discovery: on the riverbank opposite the camp, upon a wrist-thick log standing vertically in the sand, wood running into anus and out through mouth and thus forcing his gaze skyward, Fu's naked and blood-covered body rested meticulously impaled.

The soldiers quickly gathered along the shore and looked on in silence, some of them trading cautious, questioning glances with their comrades, while an easterly breeze blew steadily from downriver, sending a simultaneous ruffle through Fu's blood-stiffened hair and the tree branches behind him.

Nothing to say, nothing to do: one by one, occasionally in pairs, the soldiers turned away and went back to their tents.

And quietly packed up before continuing on their way.

Do you know who did it? What difference does it make? It's done. *Do you know? Were you awake?*

What would you do if you knew who did it? *He was my friend, Wei. Yours, too.* There's nothing we can do about it now, but I promise you I did everything I could to try and stop them. *Who?* Forget it, Po. The only thing that matters now is getting where we need to go as fast as possible.

Soon after the soldiers had left the waterfall and its now sullied aura of calm, the westward trail swerved away from the river and took on a degree of steepness they'd yet to encounter during all their weeks and months of marching—so steep did it become, in fact, that strictly forward motion was no longer possible and the path was forced into a serpentine, a series of switchbacks.

The day was hot and growing hotter, and the soldiers, muttering among themselves that this can't go on for long and that the path should soon be leveling out, began shedding shirts in a futile effort to stay cool.

Their predictions, however, proved wrong, and not

only did the incline grow steadily more formidable over the hours that followed, its width decreased correspondingly as well, causing two or three tired soldiers to nearly slip and tumble down into the already traversed sections of trail below.

Without even mentioning the difficulties it caused for the horses.

And still the situation worsened: having narrowed and steepened to such a degree that several soldiers had begun feeling the first faint stirrings of vertigo, the path then shot off from the ground and continued along a bamboo ladder that rose seemingly without end up the mountainside.

The consistently increasing gradient had reached its logical culmination: sheer verticality, a cliff.

Risky for the men, impossible for the horses.

Ensued a discussion regarding the best way to proceed:

Abandon the horses? abandon the mission?

There's starvation behind us and god knows what ahead.

Duty to ourselves or duty to the nation?

The latter doesn't matter if we end up dying anyway.

We've already come this far; the top can't be much farther—just shimmy on up and see what we find?

How many hours left of daylight?

Don't want to find yourself climbing up that thing in the darkness.

Send up a small team while the others stay and wait?

Agreed.

Keep the horses, the bulk of the supplies, and if we're not back by tomorrow evening, assume the worst.

And so, although they would have preferred a better understanding of the structural specifics keeping it affixed to the cliff, Po, Wei, Anching, and Fuzhi set off up a makeshift ladder of unknown origin.

The four young soldiers made a short-lived show of confidence as they took their first steps up the cliff, but they were quickly overcome by terror as the distance between ground and rung expanded to potentially life-threatening heights.

Born and bred on the flattest of plains, mountains and hills acting only as backdrop, this was an undertaking that sat far outside anything they'd yet experienced . . .

But they forged on ahead, their eyes directed always upward so as to keep the ever-increasing nothingness that lay below them as far from their minds as possible, and, eventually—pointless to even guess how long: fear had distorted time more than a bullet does a face—they reached the ladder's last rung and pulled themselves up onto a tauntingly narrow ledge where they then found themselves faced with yet another ladder.

Having already exerted a great deal of effort on the ascent thus far, they started up the second ladder with no small amount of reluctance, their backpacks becoming increasingly onerous with every rung that passed under their feet.

A second ledge, this one charitably spacious, was reached in a shorter amount of time than it'd taken to reach the first—or perhaps time had just contracted back to normality—but, once again denied a horizontal means of progression, the four heaving soldiers dropped their packs to the ground and their bodies into a squat, just a five-minute rest and then we'll be back on our way.

A rest that naturally strayed beyond the agreed-upon time limit, the soldiers only finding the will to go on when Anching remarked that the daylight seemed to be swiftly disappearing.

But first was raised the question of whether or not it might be best to leave the packs on the ledge and finish the climb unburdened.

A short discussion brought about a simple solution: two bags would be taken and two left behind, someone's going to have come back down anyways, this way we'll at least have some supplies if we decide to spend the night up there—so Po and Wei trudged on with their backpacks, a compromise having been reached that the responsibility would be shifted for the rest of the climb.

A compromise, however, that proved unnecessary: a relatively short climb sufficed to bring them to a large expanse of level ground, whereupon lay a path leading away from the cliff and into a spacious grove filled with breeze-blown elm trees.

The four soldiers let out a spontaneous celebratory cheer, but their mood just as spontaneously dampened when they turned back to the ladder to admire the view and instead were reminded of the fact that at least one of them—if not all four—would have to once again confront the ladder, the fact that this time gravity would now be pulling in their favor doing little to render the prospect more palatable.

But not tonight, oh no, not tonight . . .

Such was the sentiment thought and then voiced by the four exhausted members of the Western Contingent, leaving them with the rest of the evening to explore their surroundings.

They followed the path into the grove, the late afternoon light coming down pleasantly through the leaves, and within minutes came to a shallow creek; no bridge in sight, so they removed boots, hiked up pants, and went straight through the water; and then, having crossed, continued on their way barefoot, the soft, almost rockless trail powdering their road-weary feet with a soothing layer of cool dirt.

Minutes later there appeared in the distance, visible through the spaces between the trees, a solitary wooden building sitting to the left of the path.

The four soldiers drew their guns and approached with caution, eyes beating back and forth between the building and the forest.

But as they neared the structure, their fear subsided: it was clearly a temple, and if there was anyone you could trust not to shoot at you amid the war and famine and general chaos, it was a monk.

Still, better not to take any chances.

They shouted out a greeting so as not to take anyone by surprise and, when there was no response, let themselves in and made a thorough inspection of the interior, of the courtyard, of the monk's chambers, even of the space behind the incense altar.

Then one of the surroundings, during which, to the soldiers' delight, a diverse and bountiful garden was discovered just steps away from the temple's rear exit.

No sign of threat either inside or out, though the absence of monks did seem somewhat peculiar—they did some half-hearted theorizing, Fuzhi suggesting that they might be on a pilgrimage, Po countering that surely they would have left someone behind to look after the place, but truth be told, they weren't particularly concerned: they had a temple built to house dozens of monks at their disposal and a variety of food such as they hadn't seen since the banquet in Duaiyang.

For at least one night, they would sleep indoors; for at least one night, they would have fresh food.

While Anching went off to gather firewood, the

three other soldiers made their way gleefully through the garden, gathering up vegetables and fruits both familiar and exotic—and, for a moment, numbed by excitement for the coming meal, Po forgot about the violent fate met by his friend, earlier that very day; upon realizing his mental lapse, Po mutely scolded himself and interrupted his foraging to look at Wei, who returned his stare with an obnoxiously cheerful smile.

Eggplant? *I already picked some.*

And so they cooked and then they feasted, lamenting only the fact that all the alcohol was back with the horses.

And after eating entered into the inevitable discussion regarding who would go back down the ladder tomorrow and what should we tell the others?

On the latter issue they reached an easy consensus: they would continue forward, the surviving members had enough collective backpack space to take most of the supplies now being carried by the horses, and going back through the famine-afflicted territories could only bring about trouble.

As for the former, Po and Wei claimed exemption for having carried the packs up the third ladder.

A fair point agreed upon by all, which left the issue to be sorted out between Anching and Fuzhi—Fuzhi cited age-based seniority, while Anching, after several minutes of deliberation, was unable to dredge up anything with which to counter Fuzhi's argument.

So, of the four brave soldiers, two passed the night in deep, peaceful, climbing-induced slumber, whereas the other two tossed and turned and caught only fleeting moments of sleep, one dreading a second confrontation with the ever-extending ladders, the other kept up by grief and obsessive reimaginings of his friend's final moments.

The next morning, Fuzhi, Po, and Wei accompanied

Anching back to the ladder to see him off, wishing him luck and telling him to be back before nightfall, and then returned to the temple.

They spent several hours relaxing and idly exploring the space between the temple and the cliff, but after lunch—the months of marching having instilled in them a need for movement—they began to feel a nagging restlessness and found themselves walking aimlessly from one place to another only to return to where they'd started, their eyes aimed almost always in the direction of the ladder, their ears eager to receive any aural evidence of their comrades' approach.

In the midafternoon they competed with each other in a series of footraces for no other reason than to vent their excess energy, and when they noticed soon after that the sun was already on its way down, panic took a firm grip of them as the realization set in that their comrades would likely not be arriving on time.

They hurried to the ladder and took turns squinting down it, shouting out hellos or names or just short meaningless yelps.

But: there was no response, and less than an hour later the three soldiers were back at the temple, cooking a simple dinner—beneath a trim waxing moon—that none of them had any real appetite for.

And, as they'd all secretly suspected would be the case—the months of marching having instilled in them an expectation for unfavorable outcomes—there was no sign of their comrades the day after, or the day after that.

They've abandoned us.

They ought to have at least sent someone up to get us.

Or: maybe Anching wanted revenge for being sent down alone and told them something happened to us.

Or: maybe they were ambushed and now they're dead, like all the others.

But: what difference does it make to us now?

On their fourth morning at the temple, the three brave soldiers decided it was time to move on and, after Fuzhi and Po had gone down the ladder to recover the two abandoned backpacks—which they were grateful and somewhat surprised to find still resting on the ledge—they packed away as many vegetables and fruits as they could manage and then continued on their mission toward the west.

Shortly after leaving the temple, they saw an unidentifiable mass up ahead in the middle of the path; ever cautious, the soldiers slowed their pace, drew their weapons, and as they came nearer saw that the first mass was followed by other similarly shaped masses scattered here and there farther up the trail, and that the first mass was, in fact, the decomposing and disrobed body of a monk.

The soldiers, by now inured to this kind of thing, had no real emotional reaction to speak of, but still, the smell . . .

Wei estimated that he'd been dead for at least a week, likely longer.

Which neither Fuzhi nor Po saw any reason to refute, and so the three soldiers hurried on their way, glancing obliquely at the bodies until they'd passed what appeared to be the final one.

Fourteen in total, according to Wei.

Not that it made any difference to the remaining members of the Western Contingent.

The path remained mercifully level for the rest of the morning but developed a sudden and taxing gradient just as the sun began sending down its stronger midday rays.

And, further dampening morale, above the trees

they could now make out a looming wall of rock in the near distance, another obstruction to horizontal movement sitting atop the small mountain they thought they'd already conquered.

They thus spent the next hour in wretched suspense, imagining more ladders, more obstacles, a never-ending rise into the void . . .

But their fears proved to be unfounded: the path again leveled out and then made an easy detour around the cliff, and when the soldiers reached the other side they saw that before them awaited an easy descent down a shrub-speckled, nearly treeless slope, which then flattened out into an arid plain that stretched away into what may as well have been infinity.

Villages and towns of varying size sat irregularly spaced over the sand-colored expanse of land; to the south, the Sanyi could be seen winding its way back toward some distant point of origin; and to the south of the Sanyi, lining the horizon, snowcapped mountaintops hovered in stark juxtaposition to the unclouded sky.

Sighs of relief from the three brave soldiers.

We must be getting close. We can it make down before evening if we're fast enough.

And so they were, the spacious trail, gentle slope, and wide switchbacks allowing them to build up a comfortable momentum and jog their way down off the mountain and onto the plain, where, elated at the great leap forward they felt they'd made, they built a campfire and, after a large meal of temple-grown vegetables, pitched a single tent and fell swiftly to sleep.

They'd come over a mountain—from here on out, things would be strictly horizontal.

But their soothing abstract dreams of even surfaces and one-hundred-and-eighty-degree angles were intruded upon when, well before daybreak, Fuzhi rushed abruptly out of the tent and, with barely enough time to pull down his pants, sent the contents of his bowels splattering out over the ground.

Sweating and moaning, he remained squatting for several minutes while his arms roamed up and down over his midsection in a vain search for abdominal relief.

Wei and Po went outside to offer him water, but he waved them impatiently away, claiming he didn't need it and that I feel better now anyway.

The three soldiers then went back to bed, only to be awakened at least twice more during the night by Fuzhi's gastrointestinal affliction.

By morning, however, Fuzhi's health seemed to have improved, and the soldiers were able set off in the direction of the Sanyi.

But soon thereafter, last night's campsite still well within shouting distance, Fuzhi's face took on a patchy and pallid complexion and rivulets of sweat began streaming down from his hairline; after once again reassuring his comrades that he was fine, he casually asked them if they felt at all cold and then, before they'd had a chance to answer, rushed off to the side of the trail to once again relieve himself.

As he came walking unsteadily back, Po and Wei suggested, insisted even, that they take a rest, but Fuzhi insisted in turn that they carry on, that after each release his strength felt fully restored and that there was no point in them losing time because of a minor—but his sentence was cut short as he rushed back off to the side of the trail to once again relieve himself.

Po and Wei repitched the tent and, despite his protests, demanded that Fuzhi lie down inside it.

What do you think's wrong with him? *I don't know, maybe something he caught on the mountain.* We've been eating the same food as him, drinking the same water, sleeping in the same places. What if we get sick, too? *Relax, okay? He just needs to rest.*

Throughout the remainder of the early morning, Fuzhi was sent crawling outside at roughly half-hour intervals by his spasm-seized entrails, and by midmorning, when he'd taken to vomiting as well, said intervals began shrinking with alarming rapidity.

In the early afternoon, after deciding that he felt most comfortable in the sunshine and then lying for hours outside on top of his sleeping bag, squirming and feverish and drifting in and out of consciousness, sending shit into his pants and bile out over his uniform in between lengthy rambling soliloquies about his recently deceased grandmother, Fuzhi finally succumbed to whatever it was that'd been ailing him.

Po and Wei—hopefully considering the possibility that Fuzhi hadn't really died and might pop up off the ground at any given moment, revitalized and radiant with life force—took their time packing up the tent, every now and then glancing over at their comrade's filth-coated, motionless body.

He's dead. I know.

And so the two remaining members of the Western Contingent started back on their way in a solemn silence, the mountain base to their left providing them with continual confirmation that they were indeed heading south in the direction of the Sanyi, and when the sun at last vanished behind the snowcapped mountains, the two old friends wordlessly set up camp before sitting down to a difficult to digest meal of dried fish.

The vegetables, now seen as a potential source of sickness, having been discarded many hours earlier.

They woke up before sunrise the next morning, restless and ready to carry on with their journey, and, after a hasty and haphazard packing away of their tent, walked for well over an hour by the light of the moon; they stopped to watch when the sun first appeared in the east and began shedding its light out over the plain but—underwhelmed by what they'd been expecting to give them a kick of enthusiasm, of inspiration, of patriotism, of anything—almost immediately decided that they were wasting their time and carried on walking . . .

No more than an hour later, there materialized in the distance what seemed to be a large band of travelers moving perpendicular to the two soldiers, in a roughly westerly direction—meaning, Po surmised, that the path would soon be turning to follow the course of the Sanyi.

A binocular-assisted examination of the group gave cause for concern: some fifty or sixty oddly dressed men—all shouldering rifles—were accompanied by about a dozen horses and, trailing at the rear, about a dozen chained and emaciated women.

Also up ahead, the soldiers now noticed, was a structure in an advanced state of ruination—maybe a fortress, maybe a remnant of an ancient city wall—that sat at a steadily increasing distance from the peripatetic gun-toters.

Do you see that horse near the back? I think so. *At the very back, the last one.* Yeah. *Isn't that one of ours?* I can't tell from here.

Wei and Po slowed their pace, came to an almost total halt, waited until even through binoculars the group had grown indistinct—a unified monotone mass fading into the distance—and then continued forward.

The structure—which they saw upon closer inspection was indeed an open-air fortress, simple in design, a crumbling circular enclosure that in both color and texture matched its rocky reddish-yellow surroundings—was tucked between a fork in the road whose two branches led in opposite directions along the edge of a shallow canyon carved out by the Sanyi.

The two soldiers stared at the path leading

downriver and wondered aloud where it could go, is it possible that we missed something and could have just gone around the mountain?

Entering the fortress, they were given something close to an answer: Lihuang's body, still in uniform, lay prone in the dirt near the structure's midpoint, his eyes directed in their general direction, his back shot through with a series of bullets.

Beyond Lihuang's corpse, near the far wall of the fortress, there was a wagon-sized patch of what looked like freshly disturbed dirt; as Po and Wei moved closer, they saw two rootlike growths curling up out of the half of the patch nearest to them and, at the farther end, something that looked like an oversized piece of ginger.

And then, coming still closer, they saw that the former was in fact a pair of fingers, and the latter the upper half of a hand.

They recalled the oft repeated rumors that a

propensity for live burials had spread among certain warlords and came to the obvious conclusion.

But what about Lihuang? Who knows, I'd rather be shot than buried, though.

Nothing to do, no more to be said.

They left the fortress, waited a short while to give the group that had presumably murdered their comrades a little more space, and then started back toward the west.

Although feeling now aimless.

And wondering whether or not their purported destination really existed.

And whether or not the two of them were any kind of substitute for the forty-eight soldiers that were purportedly expected there.

They walked on for several more days, bypassing

villages and avoiding anyone they saw coming toward them on the path, sleeping in hard-to-reach places that stray travelers or bandits were unlikely to stumble upon.

Surveying the landscape through binoculars, they would sometimes catch clear glimpses of the local architecture or the local faces, both of which seemed somehow, though not entirely, foreign.

They began mulling over the possibility of turning around and trying their luck back at the abandoned temple and its generous garden, we could spend the summer there, wait for the famine to run its course—and be back in Luan by autumn.

They would come to a full stop at the center of the path, sure of their decision, of the soundness of their plan, but then—wondering if their destination might be just another day away, who knows, maybe just another hour—they would talk themselves into continuing upriver and around the next bend.

This cycle of decision-making was repeated several times a day for several days in a row, and only came to an end when, early one evening, after a long, barren, lifeless stretch of path, they came to a thin bridge made of rope and wood sagging precariously over the Sanyi, near whose entrance was a toppled-over metal pole—at one end of which was a crumpled and mud-matted liberationist flag.

Shifting their eyes toward the opposite side of the river, to the point where the bridge would lead them, the soldiers saw a large looming building backlit by the setting sun.

Prudence forced them to make a slow, impatient crossing over the less than confidence-inspiring bridge—its faded wooden planks creaking under each careful step—and when they were back at last on solid ground and able to focus on something other than the placement of their feet, they saw yet another flagpole, erect, tall, on which, hoisted to the highest point possible, was yet another liberationist flag.

The building behind the flag was unlike any the two soldiers had ever before encountered: metal, massive, windowless as far as they could tell, and with a gaping black entrance cut out of the wall nearest the path.

Owing to the light, they could make out only the most indistinct of shapes inside.

They shouted out a series of greetings, of liberationist slogans—silence, and so they moved cautiously toward the entrance, guns drawn.

Nearing the building's threshold, they saw that it did, in fact, have windows, two rows of them running along the upper edges of the walls perpendicular to the entrance and through which enough light entered to give the two young soldiers some idea of what was contained within.

They stepped inside, found piles and piles of overturned crates, all of them seemingly empty, most of them labeled in a script they were unable to pronounce, let alone understand.

Dust floated up through the shafts of light falling down upon the mess.

There was a noise to their right.

Two haggard figures stood behind an especially large crate in the nearest corner of the building, pistols drawn and pointed at the two remaining members of the Western Contingent.

Wei, without a word, began firing.

FOUR

Po RESTED NEAR the top of the steep slope that led down into the Sanyi, sometimes lying out on his side, sometimes doing his best to sit up, or even to crawl toward the bridge, although what the bridge might possibly do for him now he couldn't say; he wondered why he didn't feel more pain; he wondered why, with all the blood he seemed to have lost, he was still breathing; occasionally, when he wearied of staring out at the water, he turned his head and retraced with his eyes the blood-smeared groove he'd carved out in the dirt while dragging his body from the building to the river's edge; regarding Wei's death, he felt nothing; regarding the bullets he was responsible for putting into at least one of the squatters' bodies—his first direct contribution to the death of another person during all his time as a soldier—he felt a slight tinge of remorse; he wondered why the cold didn't seem to bother him; he wondered what the colonel was doing, wondered if he was alive; occasionally, when he wearied of staring out at the water or the blood-smeared groove leading back to the building, he'd run his fingers over the wound in his thigh, or the wound in his abdomen, and wonder why he didn't feel more pain; sometime before morning, he fell unconscious; when he came to, a first band of light had appeared over the eastern horizon; he had thoughts, as anyone would, of home; then he again fell unconscious, and stayed so . . . Several days later, a small boy happened upon Po's now rotting corpse and, with a toppled-over flagpole he'd found on the other side of the bridge, succeeded in shoving the body down into the Sanyi, where it was immediately caught in the current and began floating toward the east.